Playgrounds and Ashes

Bia L. Petran

DEDICATION

To the parents who are still searching,

still aching,

still wondering.

This is for you.

You're not alone.

— Bia L. Petran

CONTENTS

1	Unwanted	1
2	Running Up the Stairs	15
3	Giggles	21
4	Forever Disney	23
5	Where the Water Splits	33
6	No Girls	39
7	The Retreat	41
8	Pink-Glazed Cakes	69
9	Cherub Curls	73

PREFACE

Why do I write about loss? Because my worst fear as a mother has always been the same: that my children might die.

For years, I have lived with that fear while caring for my three children. It came in my dreams, in my imagination, in any near-death scenarios life threw at us. Then, one day, it found its voice in stories; stories where grief could bend the universe. Where a child who disappeared in one world might still be giggling in another.

*This collection was born from fear, but also from something else: **hope**.*

Hope that the children we've lost — whether through death, memory, or time — are not really gone. That in some corner of the multiverse, they are still alive.

These stories are not real.

But they are close enough to feel real.

AUTHOR'S NOTE

This collection includes nine stories, arranged in a rhythmic pattern of 3-3-3. Three cycles of three stories each.

Each cycle contains a short story, a flash fiction, and a microfiction. The shorter pieces are meant to act as palate cleansers between the longer stories.

Cycle One begins with emotional strength and a hopeful vibe. Cycle Two explores personal identity and transformation. Cycle Three leans into nostalgia, with softer, more whimsical tones.

The themes throughout are family, loss, and haunting absence or presence.

Though rooted in personal emotions and fears, these stories are works of fiction. While some descriptions or moments are drawn from real life, all dramatic events are imagined. This is dark contemporary fiction with supernatural undertones — a space where imagination explores grief, not reality.

Content Warning: These stories contain maternal loss/imagined loss, grief, and guilt.

UNWANTED

I'm truly blessed; my life is awesome! I am grateful for my family, my house, my friends, and my career. I am strong; I am independent; I am smart and confident. Money comes easily to me from all sources.

I recite my mantra with conviction every morning. I've worked hard for all that I have. I now live in Dublin, after being raised in Connemara. Had I not moved to Dublin for college, I'd never have met Richard. Oh, lovely, reliable Richard - maybe not the wildest love I've known, but the one that's held me steady all along. We've been together for ten years. I can still see his tall, dark frame in Ivy's kitchen door. My best college friend, Ivy, whose cousin had just moved from Boston to Dublin to work for a major engineering firm. His eyes landed on mine and didn't let his gaze move from them for the rest of the night. I had charmed him that night, at Ivy's party. We swapped numbers, and we had a few dates. He was older, in his early 40s.

We got married within the year, then the kids came. Ellen is nine and Mark is five. They are the love of my life! I've been working for several companies since graduating, and I'm a successful web designer. Richard travels a lot, which means I juggle work around childcare.

I'm truly blessed; my life is awesome! I am grateful for my family, my house, my friends, and my career. I am strong; I am independent; I am smart and confident. Money comes easily to me from all sources.

It's Halloween tomorrow. I've got their costumes ready, bought off eBay for a lot of money, but only the best for my kids. I sit in the dimly lit living room, and the kids are asleep.

I suddenly hear an infant crying; it sounds as if it's coming from my kitchen. It can't be, maybe from the neighbours. Would they have someone visiting with a baby? The cry gets louder. I jolt up and walk to the kitchen. The cry gets louder and louder as I approach the kitchen.

I turn the handle, and I put the light on. The crying stops.

Well, strange things happen around Halloween. I

remember last year, I got so scared seeing a child's shadow in the hallway. I froze on the spot, but it turned out to be Richard's travel bag with a coat on top of it. We had a good laugh about it.

I go upstairs to bed. I settle in, listening to relaxing meditation music from my phone. I drift to sleep.

I dream of a hospital room full of baby cots, those ugly metallic hospital ones. There's a baby in each cot, and the room seems never-ending; it's like a long corridor full of sleeping babies. I peer into one cot, smiling at the chubby baby who's sleeping there. I blink, and suddenly I see a skull where the chubby cheeks were before. I recoil and stumble over another cot. I fall and shriek. All the babies start crying. I wake up.

At the same moment, Ellen's scream pierces the night. I rush to her room. She's sitting up, drenched in sweat, with wide eyes pointing at her wardrobe. "Mom, Mom, someone was just there!"

"It was a dream, honey, there's nobody there," I say soothingly.

"Mom, there was a boy around my age who was screaming and swearing at me. He hates me. He was saying *It should have been me, not you!*

over and over again."

I frown. What does that dream mean? But then, Ellen always had weird dreams. I settle her back to sleep, and I nod off in her bed too.

The next day, at the office, my laptop keeps turning on and off by itself. I get IT to look at it. There's nothing they can see, it all seems to be working fine. But then, once I start typing, it turns off again.

At home, later on, my TV goes off and on again without me touching the remote. How strange, it must be a power surge, but why both at home and in the office??

I switch the TV off, better safe than sorry. When the image goes, there's a flicker of a child's shadow on the screen, like the black and white dots from olden times. The child has a huge head and warped limbs, like there's something wrong with him. He looks around Mark's age. I've seen that child before. I had a few nightmares with that shape of a child, like a malformed one. This is all very strange.

On Halloween evening, I go trick-or-treating with the kids happily sauntering in front of me around our estate. There are so many kids around! One of them catches my attention. She is wearing a red cape and red flowers around her pretty hair. She looks much older than Ellen, and she is alone. I keep seeing her staring at me. She looks familiar, her dark hair and blue eyes are familiar to me, but I don't know from where. "Hi," I say, smiling at her when she gets a bit closer.

She never replies. She keeps following us from a distance, just walking and hiding in the bushes. This is one strange child, I think and shrug. Not my business. I turn around later, and she's gone.

That night, Halloween night, I dream of her. Of that perfect, beautiful girl who looks at me with such love, more even than Ellen. "Who are you?" I ask her in the dream.

"I'm Obsession," she says. "I wanted to come to you and Luke, but you chased me away."

I wake up with a fright.
Luke was the first person I ever loved like that - a young painter with long, dark hair and blue eyes. Our love burned intensely for a whole summer, then we split up. It scared me how intense it was; it scared him, too. I had discovered I was pregnant in October, and I had an abortion. I didn't even tell him. Wow, I haven't thought of that in years! Why now?

Cora comes over for coffee. Cora is my elderly

neighbour, who is so kind to the kids and me! She's become a good friend. She invites Ellen over, and they talk and bake together. She is spiritual, into crystals and angels. She always gets Ellen to pick an angel card. At first, I didn't like that, but it can't harm Ellen. The energy in Cora's house is so peaceful and calm, just like her eyes. I tell her about my dream, about the abortion. I don't know why. I usually don't share personal things. But she came over unannounced as if she felt I needed her.

She tells me that there's an unborn realm, where unborn babies live forever. "Maybe there's something she needs to tell you," she says. "Just be open to messages from that world."

This scares me a bit. I don't like to be out of control. I ring Richard, and he laughs in my face. "Jeez, you see a girl in a red cape at Halloween everywhere. And a dream is just a dream." He knows about my abortions, he knows about all four of them.
My first one was when I was seventeen, with my first-ever boyfriend from secondary school back in Carraroe. We both stole money from our parents and went up North for the abortion. We got back the same day, and we couldn't be out at night at that age. We both agreed we didn't want the baby; we were kids ourselves. I never had any regrets over it.

My second one was at twenty with my Luke. That one broke my heart. I cried for months after, wishing to still hold Luke in my arms, also knowing it wouldn't have worked.

My third pregnancy happened from a one-night stand in Carlow. I was drunk, and I wasn't careful. It was a clear choice for an abortion. Again, no regrets.

And then a fourth one was with Richard. We got married really fast, and we both decided we wanted to be together for a few years before having kids, to have some fun and travel. That one was a bit frustrating, and it felt different from the others because I was married. That was when I told him I had had three other abortions, as we needed to make a decision, knowing all the facts. He was nice and tender afterwards, and I recovered fast. We travelled to Thailand the following week, and we had a blast!

I'm truly blessed; my life is awesome! I am grateful for my family, my house, my friends, and my career. I am strong; I am independent; I am smart and confident. Money comes easily to me from all sources.

I book a session with Diane, my therapist. I share

about the abortions and how I'm thinking of them now for some reason. She tells me ghosts and spirits don't exist, and that the realm Cora mentioned isn't real. She gets me to focus on the now, on what I have, do some grounding exercises, and let go of the past. She is pretty cold, and when I leave her office, I get a shiver down my spine.

One day, Ellen shows me a bruise on her shoulder. She says the angry boy who visits her at night gave it to her. I freak out. Does she need therapy? I ring her teacher, and she tells me that no, no incidents had happened at school.
That night, a boy came to me in my dream. He looks somehow familiar. "I'm Rage," he says. "I did punch your girl. Why didn't you have me?" He shouts at me angrily, pushing me with force, throwing me into the wall behind. "You and Dad are criminals. I hate you both! You killed me, but you had two more kids then! I hope you die," he says and disappears.
I wake up and hear a whisper in the dark, "Don't mind him, Mommy, I love you so much! I'm Obsession. All I want is for you to hold me, please hug me!" I switch the light on, and there's nobody in my room.

I start putting on my makeup for the day. I look down to choose my lipstick, and when I look back up, I see a child in the mirror. He's looking at me coldly, and he is wearing a black Metallica t-shirt with the word *Distance* written across the top of it. He shrugs, and then he disappears. Wait a minute, I've seen that shirt before! A flicker of memory, a packed pub in Carlow and a hot dude in a Metallica t-shirt…us riding on his motorbike back to his apartment…us having steamy, drunken, messy sex…. Now I know who the child is - it's from my one-night stand.

I try to make sense of it all. I need my Emma, my bestie. We book a meal, and we open a bottle of wine. I tell her what I think, my aborted kids are reaching out to me from their world. Emma is a no-nonsense doctor; she doesn't believe in spirits. She thinks I'm having a nervous breakdown. "Take a break from work," she says, "go to a spa or a retreat. You're going crazy. Are you still going to therapy?" she asks.

I say, "No, I don't like to go anymore!" She makes me promise I'll start going again. She tells me to ring her day or night if I need anything.

Every night I'm dreaming of the kids….Rage, Obsession, Distance (that's what I call him). There's another one, the oldest one, who appeared twice in my rear-view mirror and almost made me crash the car. I call that one Pain, as his face is always scrunched up as if in pain.

But almost every second day, I see the malformed one as a shadow, with twisted limbs and a huge head, looking somehow like an octopus. Who is that? I had four abortions, then I had Ellen. It suddenly dawns on me. The miscarriage! The baby we lost in between Ellen and Mark. Could that baby have been malformed, and that's why I miscarried? I remember the pain. Physical and psychological. When I chose not to have babies, I didn't feel much guilt. But when I miscarried, I was desperately heartbroken. Having no choice made that a different experience.

I'm truly blessed; my life is awesome! I am grateful for my family, my house, my friends, and my career. I am strong; I am independent; I am smart and confident. Money comes easily to me from all sources.

I feel watched every day. I hear strange sounds all around me that nobody else hears. I hear footsteps up the stairs, I see the kids' faces in mirrors, in smoke shapes, in cloud shapes…. They are all around me. I feel they are suffocating me. "What do you want from me?" I shout to the sky.

I'm home alone, as Richard took the kids to his mom's for the week. I finish my wine glass. I nod off on the sofa. I wake up in the darkness and go upstairs. I enter Ellen's room and turn on the light. Her pink walls look black now; her cheerful paintings are black and grey. Her dolls have blood coming from their eyes. They start laughing and singing, and crying, the noise is horrendous. I cover my ears and run to Mark's room. It's got a vortex in the middle, and I fall through it. I land in a twisted playground, but everything has ugly metal spikes. Dark blood covers the monkey bars. The black roundabout spins by itself, creaking with a high-pitched metallic squeal. The sandpit isn't filled with sand, but with a thick red good that is bubbling.

Rage appears and pushes me down a spiky slide. I feel the spikes tearing my legs and buttocks, I feel the burning pain.
"No!" shouts Obsession jumping off an upside-down swing, and she slaps Rage.
"Oh, Mommy," she says, cuddling me in her arms. She shouts at Distance, "Hey, help me!" He just stares and says, "I don't care."

I feel anger building up, mixing with my pain, and I shout at Rage, "Stop hurting my Ellen, stop hurting my girl!"
"Or what?" he asks with a disgusted drawl and

raised eyebrows.

Pain approaches us too, with his usual scrunched-up face, asking, "Oh, does it hurt, Mother? How much does it hurt? As much as it hurt me when you didn't want me?" His eyes are huge and shiny, full of tears.

They all gather around me and start talking and shouting at the same time, their faces inches above mine as I lie on the ground.
"Mommy, I love you, I wanna be with you!"
"Mother, I hope the wounds hurt like hell."
"I hate your guts, I hate your children."
"You know what, woman? I couldn't care less about what happens to you!"

Suddenly, they all freeze and then run. The malformed kid appears, slithering down the floor like a snake. He scared them away. "Thank you," I say. He smiles.

I wake up lying on the living room floor. How did I get here? I was upstairs in Mark's room before. I start chanting.

I'm truly blessed; my life is awesome! I am grateful for my family, my house, my friends, and my career. I am strong…

It's not working anymore! My mantra stopped working.

Every night since, I go back to the ugly playground. They surround me, they torment me. I am afraid to go to sleep, so I started taking sleeping pills to help me. I stopped meeting everyone, I stopped working, and I am isolating in the house. I asked Richard to stay at his mom's longer, lying I have some projects to deliver for work.

One morning, I look at myself in the mirror. My eyes are bloodshot, with big dark circles; my face is all blotchy and swollen. My hair is matted, sticking to my sweaty forehead. I don't recognise myself.

That night, I break down in tears, falling on my knees at the playground. "I'm sorry, I'm really sorry I killed you! Please forgive me! I love you all!"

I feel the guilt, the sorrow, and the kids' pain deep in my soul.

Obsession says, "I've forgiven you, Mommy, I love you so so much!" and she kisses my cheek.

Rage says between clenched teeth, "This is what

I wanted from you!"
Distance shrugs. "It doesn't matter!"
Pain says, "Now you feel it too!" with satisfaction in his voice.
The malformed one just smiles at me.

I wake up. I go to the bathroom cabinet, and I take out the small white box. The pregnancy test I got Emma to buy for me when she brought my groceries. I pee on the stick, and I wait. Tick tock! Time moves slowly.

When the time is done, I don't need to look too closely. I already know. Two lines. Positive.

Later that day, I let Cora in. I tell her I'm pregnant. "You know which one it is?" she asks gently. I nod, but I don't say the name. I am calm and hopeful.

When I fall asleep that evening, I hear a whisper, "This time, don't let me go!"

In the corner of Ellen's room, the red flower she painted on canvas at school starts to bleed.

RUNNING UP THE STAIRS

Ghosts do not exist. I've never believed in them. I always judge those who do. Like, how naive are you? They are just invented, like zombies or vampires. Stories to scare little kids.

We got a place to rent just next to the kids' new school. The owner is a burly countryside man, quite annoying, but the rent is affordable and, as I said, the location is perfect!

The house isn't great, but it's perfectly usable. A four-bedroom semi-detached brick house. Old furniture, worn-down carpets, but everything is functional. The tiny garden is overgrown and the fence is peeling, but we can fix all that.

"We're going to be happy here," I declare, opening a bottle of kiddies' champagne for us four to toast to the new place.

It's been a few weeks since we moved in. I, Dana, my husband Paul, and our two children,

Cian, aged six, and Sophia, aged ten. I am heavily pregnant with our third child. The house feels like a home now, filled with our family photos, the children's drawings, and toys. The living room looks cozy, with many bright cushions and a pink throw covering the ugly, old brown sofa. The kitchen looks better with all my utensils and gadgets strategically placed on the chipped counters.

I smile happily to myself as I look out the living room window towards the road. The school is a two-minute walk from the house. I'm expecting them back any minute. I feel the baby kicking vigorously. Oh, he's really active today. One kick to my bladder makes me go to the toilet. Ugh, there's no paper in the downstairs one. I wobble towards the stairs, and I freeze. I see a shadow. It looks like a slim teenage boy, running up the stairs, looking back at me. I realise he's not real, as the stairs always creak, and I couldn't hear a noise.

"But no, it can't be, ghosts do not exist," I mutter to myself. I am a bit scared to go upstairs, but I need to pee. The baby stopped kicking. I make my way upstairs as I hear the kids coming in downstairs through the kitchen sliding door.

After I pee, I go down and hug them tight as they chirp on about their day. I forget about the shadow.

I tell Paul about it in bed. "Your blood sugar was probably low or something," he says. "Also, you know what your imagination's like." He shrugs.

Two days later, I'm lying in bed after a daytime nap, and the baby starts kicking strongly again. I'm hungry, so I go down to the kitchen. The doorbell rings. As I walk towards the front door, I see the same shadow of a boy running up the stairs. I freeze. The doorbell rings again.

I open it. It's my neighbour Camilla. We have tea together, and I tell her about my sightings.

She sighs. She tells me there was a family from Nigeria that lived in the house four years ago. They were lovely, they had four children aged three to seventeen. Their oldest boy got involved with drugs and gangs, and the parents were desperate. The police were constantly at their door. The dad was very strict. He threw the boy out on the street one night. The wife and he had a big fight that evening. She didn't agree with him kicking the boy out.

The next day, they rang all their son's friends they knew of, and they went looking for him in his usual hanging places. They didn't find him. They declared him missing. He was never found.

Camilla says she had watched the dad get more and more quiet and grumpy, drowning his guilt into whiskey bottles. They really couldn't handle what happened, and two years later, they moved back to Nigeria.

Camilla expresses her belief that the boy had died and found his way home now, after all these years, and he is looking for his family. His name was Lucas.

I am not sure I believe this, but then, I saw him twice.

I say all this to Paul, who laughs in my face again. "Stop it," he says over dinner.

"Stop what?" asks Sophia, who came into the kitchen to bring a bowl I gave her with cut apples.

"Nothing, darling," I say sweetly.
"No, I heard you. Were you talking about the teenage boy?" she asks.

"I never said teenage," I say, "I just said boy."
"I know, Mommy, but I saw him a lot of times. He just stares at me, then runs up the stairs. He's probably going to his room. My room was his, you know?" she says in her sweet little lilting voice.

I freeze. Paul stops eating. We don't know what to say. Sophia giggles. "He's a friendly guy, don't worry. He's just looking for his family."
"They moved back to Nigeria," I say.
"Ok, Mommy, I'll tell him," she says.

"Wait, do you speak to him?" I ask, now truly frightened.

"No, but I just know it. I dreamt of his family, and I dreamt of my room when it was his. It had a big TV and an Xbox by the window, and the bed was on the other side. He had a shelf of trophies and books," she says.

I don't like this. I don't know what to say. "Honey, ghosts aren't real," Paul says.

"But Mommy AND I saw him!" she shouts.

I feel the baby kicking energetically again.

I hear Sophia happily in the hallway: "Hey, my Mommy says your family moved to Nigeria." At exactly that moment, my water breaks all over the kitchen floor. *It's too early*, I think, half excited, half scared.

"OMG, we need to run to the hospital," Paul says, panicking. He rings Camilla to come and mind the kids while we go to the hospital.

I turn around in circles, not knowing what to grab or take. I don't have a bag organised; it's only thirty-three weeks...

The baby is born seven weeks early, a healthy baby boy. Lucas.

From that day, neither I nor Sophia saw the black teenage boy running up the stairs again.

GIGGLES

Since they got married and moved to the new house, they had been hoping. Monthly hopes, always crashing in a wave of tears. Many years passed by.

Sometimes Anna dreams of them. A girl with long, blonde hair and huge, blue eyes, and a gap-toothed boy with scratched knees. Scenes of bliss, of happy horseplaying with her and Adam, him twirling the girl up in the air, her kissing the sweaty hair of the boy. They always look the same, sound the same.

She hears them giggle sometimes, when she sits in the conservatory. Before falling asleep, she sees glimpses of them, she hears feet up the staircase, she smells the toast from their cartoon plates, she sees the spilled juice from their cups. She shares this with Adam, bracing herself for him to mock her. Adam doesn't believe in what doesn't exist.

To her surprise, Adam's eyes light up. "I thought it was just me. I didn't want to tell you after seeing how upset you got every month. I see them too, I hear them too," he says. "I hear them the most from the conservatory, or just before falling asleep. I dream about them too, and we are always in this house."

"Do you think they exist?" I ask him.
"Yes, they do exist, somewhere, just not here," he says staring blankly into the distance.

"Be happy, our little angels, be happy wherever you are," they whisper, holding hands and looking through the conservatory door to the garden outside. The shining sun makes the sliding glass door look almost like a mirror.

From the other side of the glass, two voices whisper back, "We are happy, we love you, other mom and dad."

And two kids, a girl with long blond hair and huge blue eyes, and a gap-toothed boy with scratched knees, run into the conservatory to play with their toys that are strewn all around.

FOREVER DISNEY

It's 2025. It's James's turn to go to Disneyland Paris with us. His brothers and sister had already gone a few times. The last time was back in 2014 for David's 10th birthday. Back then, James was only one, so he got left behind with Granny Alexa.

James is twelve now. He has never forgotten about being left behind. It's his turn now! He's excited mainly for the Star Wars and Marvel rides. Also, it's cool to just be the single child for a few days, and not one of four fighting for the attention of the parents.

The older boys are ok; they wouldn't be interested anyway. I feel a bit guilty not taking Laura, but she is eighteen and doing her Leaving Cert this year, so she really can't miss school. We always do holidays outside the school ones, especially short four-day ones like this one. But I see how excited James is, and also John needs a break from his stress at work, and especially from his new manager, who is an asshole.

This will be nice, I think, starting to relax, sipping from my cheap champagne in a plastic cup on the flight to Paris.

We get there, and we check into Newport Bay, the same Disney hotel we stayed in eleven years ago. We go to bed early, as we want a very early start tomorrow.

It's April, it's sunny but there are some clouds too; perfect weather for an Irish family not used to the hot weather. The Parks are buzzing with excited kids and adults. The cheerful shrieks, the tantrums, the stressed-looking parents, it's the same as always. We go straight to the Avengers Campus and do some of the rides there. We hate queuing, so we jump from place to place before finally settling in a queue. We do the Spiderman shooting ride three times, and then a few more of the Avengers rides.

John and I stop at the RC Racer. James doesn't want to go on. "I'll stay with him," I say, a bit disappointed as I want to go on this one. I didn't do it last time, and I want to do all the rides in Disneyland, except for the Indiana Jones one that still scares me.
John says James will be ok to wait here for us. "Won't you, James?" he asks. He points at a low

wall where he can wait for us. "Do not move from here," we tell him in our strictest tones. "We won't be long as there isn't a queue."

I throw one last hesitant look towards the place we left him, just in front of the Slinky Dog Zig Zag Spin we had come off after doing it three times. James also had his phone, so we could be in contact if needed. Plus, he was almost thirteen! He'll be fine!

We get off the ride still buzzing with adrenaline, laughing and walking hand in hand. John loves the faster and more dangerous rides, so this was nothing for him, but I really enjoyed it. We walk fast towards the place where we left James. "Slow down," John laughs.
I know that I have my "worried face" on, as he always says, but I can't shake a feeling of unrest.

We get there. No James. We look around, thinking he's just hiding to scare us. I ring his phone. It is off. This is worrying. I look around, and I see an area between some trees where you can go via a path onto another area of the park. "What if someone has taken him, John?" I shout. John doesn't look worried. "How can you not even care?" I snap at him angrily, pushing him slightly. "He's fine," John says. "Maybe he went to do the Slinky again." I look at him. He's as calm as always, just casually looking around him.

We rush over; we check the queue, the cars, and there's no James.

I am starting to hyperventilate. Then I say, "Let's go to the parachute ride, he loved that one." Sure, there James was, having the time of his life, beaming from ear to ear, flying up and down with his curls flapping in the wind.

I hug him hard, and he shrugs out of it. "Moooom!" he goes, embarrassed as some little girls were looking at us.
"James, this is serious. We told you not to move!" I start.
"Well, you were taking too long," he chirps and walks away.

He is at that teenage stage where they get rebellious. It's truly a heart attack waiting to happen for me. John is annoyingly calm all the damn time; he gets on my nerves. Compared to him, I look like a crazy, paranoid woman.

We enjoy the rest of the day and evening with no other bad events. "It's been a heck of a day!" James says groggily before falling asleep in his top bunk.

On the second day, we want to do the Star Wars

ride. This used to be the Aerosmith one, my favourite ride, which I did a few times the last time we came. But only because of my love for Steven Tyler. Otherwise, you'd never had caught me doing a spin-in-the-dark rocket ride.

I insist on going on it, John also, of course, being a big Star Wars fan. James is also very excited. We queue up for forty minutes, and just before our turn comes, we get to watch how the rocket is propelled with speed.

James watches carefully, with huge eyes, then says, "Nope, I'm not doing it!" I look at his face. He is genuinely scared. Jonn starts giving out to him, trying to force him, but James says he'll just wait outside. I don't feel ok doing this, but then our turn just comes up, so we move forward. We shout, "Now careful, don't go anywhere like last time." We don't hear his reply as we get into the rocket.

We do the ride, and we get out. We don't see him. *Not again*, I think. Then we realise we got out at a different exit, so we run around, and we look for James. It takes us a good few minutes, but we finally spot him on a bench, looking at his phone. "Oh, you scared me!" I say.

"Mom, I listened this time. No matter what I do, you're always scared and cringy! I hate you!" He shrugs my arm off. I look at John. He stays silent, he knows better than to say anything, but his eyes and his pursed lips are saying, "I told you!"

After two more rides and a hotdog pitstop, I feel James's hands around my shoulders and his sweet voice says, "I'm sorry, Mom, I don't hate you. But you must stop panicking or I will really run away!" he threatens while laughing with his hearty belly laugh I love so much. I breathe in the familiar smell of his hair, and all my anxiety melts off.

"Oh, I'd die without you, buddy!" I say.

We have great fun for the rest of the day, and again we sleep early, ready for another day of fun. All the walking has us falling into bed the minute we get to the room. We had wanted to get some cocktails downstairs, but we are much too tired.

On the third day, we go to Walt Disney Studios, we do some stuff there, and then James says, "I wanna explore by myself for a bit. I know the two parks now, just give me my ticket and we can meet at the Cartoons place, that cinema in one hour."

"No fucking way!" I start. But John says, "Sure, dude". I frown at him, and he goes "He's gonna be thirteen, you must cut the umbilical cord already!"

I say, "I get it, but there are thousands of people here, who knows what can happen!" "Exactly," he says, "families with kids, it's all very safe here!"
"No, it's not, in big crowds that's where kidnappings happen!" I say. John hands James his ticket, and James starts walking happily towards the exit. "Let's at least follow him," I say, and we do that for a while. James walks fast, and we can't catch up with him. "Leave him," John says.

I just wanna see if he gets into the other park or goes towards the restaurants. "Oh my god, we didn't even give him some cash. It's so hot, what if he's thirsty?"
"He'll be fine for an hour," John says.
We go on the Millennium Falcon ride, but I keep scanning the crowds for James. I keep imagining the worst. *What if he got lost? What if someone kidnaps him? What if someone offers him a drink and it's laced with something?*

I've had enough. I go to the cinema and find a seat where I can watch the door from. It's only been half an hour. It felt like four full hours. John went to do the Star Wars ride again.

I wait and wait. I badly need the toilet, but I'm scared to go in case I miss James coming in. I go outside and take a good look. Nothing.

I go back in, and I see the back of his head in row two. How did I miss him earlier? I go closer and just as I'm starting to talk to him, I see a mom with popcorn joining him. The boy turns his head. It's not James.

My phone rings. It's John. "Come to the Thunder Mountain quickly," he says, in a panicked voice that doesn't sound like him.

I rush over to the Mountain. Two cars collided, and James got hit badly. He was being taken by an ambulance when I arrived. We quickly jump in with him.

It was a long night at the hospital. But we would go home without our darling boy.

The following days are a dark blur for me. All I remember is we stayed another week, and we got his siblings to travel over too for the cremation. Our parents wanted to come, but we said not to, we just wanted to keep it to our small family.

We take his ashes and spread them around his favourite rides in Disney before going back home, heartbroken. "Disneyland will never be the same for me again, I never want to come here again, I hate this place!" I sob. This place, that I loved so much, now means only heartache to me.

John tries to console me by saying, "He will now be forever in Disneyland, the place he was so excited to go to!" I scowl at him. Not the time to be positive!
I throw the last fistful of ash up into the wind.

As we turn to leave, I hear James's voice whisper, "I love you, Mom. Come visit me here every year, please! I'll miss you!"

John insists it was just the wind. But I know what I've heard. "I will, I promise you, James!" I say into my tears.

And I intend to keep my promise.

WHERE THE WATER SPLITS

The lake still frightened her. Even after five years. Every time Alyssa passed it, avoiding looking towards it, eyes fixed firmly on the road ahead, she got a knot in her stomach and the urge to throw up, her fingers tightening on the steering wheel until her knuckles turned white. She could still hear her screams, she could still see Angel running towards the lifeguard hut with someone wrapped in a big towel. Alyssa was at the small kiddies pool beside the lake with her daughter Melia; Angel was in the lake with both their sons and Angel's daughter Daria.

She was trying to make out who Angel was holding in the towel, which of the three children. She quickly scooped Melia out of the water and ran towards Angel. She then saw in slow motion two kids following Angel; Angel's kids. She then knew it was Alex in that towel. Her heart stopped.

She reached the hut just as she heard the ambulance sirens. She kneeled before the shocking stillness of her five-year-old boy, devastated. She was trying not to scare Melia and the other kids, but she was heaving as the lifeguard was doing CPR on Alex. She stopped breathing. Those seconds felt like hours, but when she heard the hoarse cough and the gasping, she breathed again. She looked down, her feet were bloody, she had cut them running over rocks, but she couldn't feel a thing.

Angel was so apologetic, she had run to the toilet with Daria, and she had left the boys beside the lake on the blanket. She had no idea how Alex fell in. But she got back just as a man was pulling Alex out of the lake, and people were screaming. The kids were all in shock. We all went to the hospital, and Alex lived.

The first thing Alyssa did after the accident was to sign Alex up for swimming lessons. She couldn't have guessed back then that he would be a champion swimmer. She loves looking at the medals hanging up in his room, swollen with pride. She also loves telling the story of the accident that created this champion. Of course, Melia is also a strong swimmer now.

Still, even years later, the lake never gave her peace. They never went back to swim in it, even if they lived close by. She always said no when the kids asked to go with friends. "No, that lake tried to take you from me, Alex! I won't give it another chance!" was her permanent reply. No matter how many tears, how many threats, how many tantrums.

She hadn't meant to stop by the lake today. Alex and Melia were both asleep in the back seat, after a popcorn and Coke-fuelled cinema visit. She parked the car and walked to the edge of the lake. What made her do that? She couldn't tell, but she could feel a pull.

A woman is standing on the edge, all alone, not moving.

She looks like a statue. She seems around Alyssa's age, maybe younger. But very sad. A shadow dressed all in black, standing by the lake.

The woman looks at her with big blue pools of eyes. "I used to come here all the time," she said, "but I've stopped. Then, for some reason, I steered my car this way today," she says in a small voice.

"That's what I did too! I never stop here, but today I felt like stopping" Alyssa says. "My son drowned here five years ago this month," the woman says, like in a trance, not appearing to

have heard Alyssa.
Alyssa freezes. It is July, she realises with a squeeze of her heart.

"He was five. I only left him on the blanket for a second. A second!" the woman sobs.
Alyssa says, "My son nearly drowned here, also in July, also five years ago. But he made it," she adds, feeling guilty the minute the words left her lips. How inconsiderate of her!

The woman turns and stares at her for what feels like an eternity. It's as if she is staring into her soul. She isn't saying anything. It feels uncomfortable. Alyssa feels a knot rising in her throat.

She sighs loudly, not knowing what else to say. They keep staring at each other. It is like looking into a mirror of what could have been. Now she could see the deep lines on the woman's face, her dark circles, and her sunken cheeks.

The woman says, "I've always imagined there was another me, one that got to take him home".

Alyssa says in a tightened voice: "I've imagined the other me too. The one who didn't," she says, thinking of all the sleepless nights when she lay awake riddled in guilt.

They stand in silence for a while, two women

caught in different timelines at the edge of the lake.

And the lake stays quiet.

NO GIRLS

A story in the paper today. Two girls aged seven, raped and killed in town.

We went to the cinema with our daughters aged seven, and my son aged three. Crossing from the cinema to the shopping center, the girls running ahead, us moms chatting about the horrible news in the paper. We enter the center.

No girls. Panic washes over me.

I run to security. My friend runs to check the car.

No girls.

"Blonde girl with pink jacket, brunette girl with purple jacket. Both seven." The shopping center resonates with the announcement.

No girls.

I look for a photo of my girl on my phone for the security agent. I drop my son's hand for a second.

The radio says two girls alone were seen in Primark.

The hope. We wait for news. The security agent talks on his radio.

It's them! I breathe again.

They are bringing the girls to us. The wait seems long.

Then I remember. I look around. Where is he? We search.

The woman from the flower stall at the entrance has seen him being carried by a man and screaming. Thought it was just a spoiled toddler with a tantrum.

No boy.

THE RETREAT

This is bliss, Tara thinks, taking in the grounds of the farm. *This is just what I needed!*

She's tried, she's really tried writing at home, but with the three kids she couldn't get a minute's peace.

Luke wasn't too happy with her going. He said she didn't need the retreat as she could write in the bedroom. She tried for a whole week, but the kids kept barging in, or calling her, or texting her. How had they raised them so dependent? They can't do anything without her (even ordering one takeaway had twenty group texts…ugh)
The bus was snaking through tidy villages and fields. The retreat was in a village one hour from Nice. She looked out the window, uncomfortable in the French July heat. Fields of corn, bales of hay, fields of sunflowers. She writes short stories of idyllic romances, this is the perfect place to do it! She sighed to herself contentedly, happy she

finally chose this experience for herself.

The bus got to her stop, Châteauneuf-de-Grasse. A tiny sliver of a woman with huge hair perched on top of her head was waving at her. Angela was the owner of the retreat, an American established in France. They hugged for a moment, both excited and warm. Then they drove to the farm.
Wow, it was everything Tara imagined, a beautiful old one-storey house amid hills, and the views were amazing. There were contemplation areas cleverly spread around the grounds, there was an orchard, a forest, and an outdoor pool, all overlooking a beautiful landscape. The farmhouse was beautiful, with lovely ancient treasures of furniture and ornaments, testimony to decades long passed, but with the modern additions of today's life. The food provided was farm-to-table style, a lot of local goodness, with everything supplied from local farms. Tara was excited to swap her usually greasy diet for something grounding and healthy. She was also excited to have someone else cater for her. Angela seemed pretty mysterious, she smelled of patchouli incense, spoke in hushed, calm tones, and she had cats and dogs following her all the time.

She briefly met some of the other guests; they

were having wine outside after dinner. She mentioned she was from Ireland and writing romantic stories. The group went quiet. No one answered when she asked what they were working on.

Her commitment to herself coming to this retreat was to write a collection of twelve stories, to detoxify from the phone and social media, and to continue her journey into self-discovery by meditating, dreaming, and relaxing. She made strict rules for Luke and the kiddos. She will check the phone daily at 7 p.m. and reply to any messages then, and give them news from over here. In case there's an emergency, they can ring her, or text Angela.

She got here at 7 p.m., went to her room at 8 p.m. after a delicious steak dinner and a glass of good crisp French white wine. Even though she hadn't slept at all the night before, she found it difficult to settle down and get to sleep. She turned the light on and discovered four huge spiders in the four corners of her room; she called Angela, who arrived with three cats at her heels; she caught and released the spiders outside.

Angela had handed Tara a booklet with activities around the retreat - scheduled walks, meditation, yoga, coaching, therapy, healing sessions, Reiki etc. Tara read about them all, saying she was a bit impressed that a writing retreat has so many extra things. Angela smiled enigmatically and said in her soothing voice, "We provide what our guests need. Everyone has different needs."

Tara finally fell asleep at 2 a.m. after tossing and turning. She woke up at 4 a.m., sobbing her heart out. She thought back to her dream. Her nightmare. Falling deep inside the water, the lake's bottom calling her, pulling downwards without her resisting at all…bubbles coming out of her mouth, then she inhaled, suffocating…and then she woke up.

She got a strong impulse to ring home and check that everything's ok. But she resisted. She made these rules, she's gonna follow them!

She dozed off dreamlessly until 7 a.m. She quickly washed and went down with the thought to have a coffee and then go for a walk before the heat of the day arrived.

She saw Angela by the pool, stroking some wild rabbits and chanting something. She looks to be very in tune with nature.
She opened the kitchen door and fumbled for the light switch. "Good morning," said a man's voice from the dark. She got startled and let out a

small cry. "Oh, sorry, I didn't see you there," she laughed awkwardly. She looked at him and saw his eyes widen with ...what was that? Fear? Shock? She looked at him more carefully, they'd never met before, she was sure of it.

"Is everything ok?" she asked him, finding her customer service voice and smile.

He babbled: "But...how...what...who are you?"

She stretched her hand out and said, "I'm Tara, from Ireland, as you can probably guess from my red hair and pale skin". Ugh, why did she keep doing that? The clown in her always came out and tried to make people laugh.

"Sorry, I'm Brian, I live in Manchester. You just startled me coming in, that's all."

"What are we like?" She laughed. "The pair of us scaring each other, haha."

She made her coffee and headed purposefully to the back garden table, the designated "I don't wanna socialise" table. He stared after her. When she sat down, she saw he was still staring.

She stirred some sugar in her coffee. All of a sudden, three cats came purring towards her. One by one, crawling through the grass, jumping out from the bushes. They surrounded her and started purring against her legs. *This is very strange*, she thought. T*hey didn't react to me at all last night.*

As she'd recently dabbled in the spiritual side of things with crystals, tarot, etc, she decided to text Angela to ask for some yoga and meditation. She felt she needed that to settle her mind, as now all she thought of was the dream with the lake…and she wanted to focus on writing her beautiful stories.

As she headed back into the kitchen with her cup, she saw Brian hunched down on the floor, sobbing his heart out. She quietly put the cup down on the first surface she saw and headed out.

She walked for a while, listening to guided meditations on YouTube. But they didn't settle her as they usually do. She looked at her wrist, but her vintage watch seemed to have stopped.

Later, she got ready for the yoga and meditation session and went down by the pool, where Angela had already set out the mats. There was a cat on each mat. Tara asked her about Brian; she didn't say he cried, but she said he was acting a bit strange.
Angela told her he'd been coming to the retreat every year since 2022. His wife and three kids had died in a speedboat accident on Lake Garda back in 2019. How strange, Tara thought, we also took a speedboat on Garda, also in 2019, but nothing happened except for her freaking out

when the boys were driving and doing donuts, and they almost toppled overboard. Anyways, they all could swim except Aaron, who was only learning then, but he had a vest. Brian's story sounds like one of her "sickening imagination bouts," as her family called them. Since she was a child, Tara had had flashes of near-death experiences, potential scary outcomes, etc. She saw them vividly, not just imagined them, and then she also dreamed of them.

She felt much calmer after the yoga and meditation, she wrote a full story of forbidden love in a French village. Chuffed with herself, she sat outside under an old oak tree. An acorn fell into her lap, and she put it in her pocket.

~ Day 2 ~

The island is glistening in the rare Irish sun. What fabulous weather we are having! The hike to the Black Fort is pleasant, a bit strenuous for Tara. But Luke and the kids are sauntering ahead without a care in the world. Tara finally gets to the plateau. She sees her family in the distance, close to the edge, looking down. She calls out to them and waves at them. When she gets closer, she sees Aaron and Louise very close to the edge. She tells Luke, "Hey, be careful, pull Aaron back." Aaron is only five, and

he is a daredevil. He laughs at Mom's concern and takes another step to the edge. His sister, older by three years, copies him.
Dad is just laughing and goes "Oh, oh, guys, you're making mom mad". Their laughter grinds Tara's ears.
She starts hyperventilating; she feels a panic attack coming. She can't breathe, can't talk, she just let out a squeaky "Please, Luke!" and then falls to her knees, sobbing. "Luuuke!" He says, "Oh, stop it!" laughing again. A gust of wind suddenly makes Aaron stumble, and she watches in slow motion as Luke reaches out for him, but it is too late. She hears the crack of his head hitting the rocks below. In horror, Luke and Louise fall to their knees on the edge, looking down. "Someone call 999," shouts Luke. A startled man rings. People are starting to gather. There's screaming, there's panic… Tara is rooted to the spot; she can't move, can't go look, can't get up. She is frozen.

She woke up in a sweat. This dream again! They went to Inis Mor last year, and everything from the dream happened except for Aaron falling. She just broke down and cried, and couldn't move, so Luke and the kids had come to her and hugged her, and had said sorry for scaring her. Was she still feeding this fear so many years later? Why couldn't she forget about it? Nothing had happened after all.

Her bedside clock showed 14:12. It was impossible. Her phone said 8:00. She reset the clock to the correct time, but couldn't shake the feeling that something was happening in that room.

She got out of bed and went for a walk towards the river. She saw Maggie there, sitting on a rock, looking at the mountains in the distance. The retreat cats were all around her.

They hadn't spoken before; they just got introduced on her first day there.

"Hey, Maggie, care for some company? I can surely use some. I had a nightmare, and it unsettled me," she said.

"Sure," Maggie said, in her thick Scottish accent. "What was your nightmare about?"

"Oh, just an experience I had last year that I keep dreaming about," Tara said. "My kids were close to a cliff edge somewhere in Ireland, and I hate heights, and the fear of any of them falling was so strong. Nothing happened, thankfully, but I keep replaying it in my dreams. You know, a mother's silly fears..."

Maggie looked down, quietly wiping her eyes.

"Are you ok?" asked Tara.
"My son fell off a mountain in Austria two years ago; he was only 6. Mountain rescue came, but they couldn't do anything. He was our only child. It destroyed us. Mike and I split up as we handled our grief in different ways. I blamed him! I still do, he encouraged Johnny to get close to the edge, he wanted to raise him like a real man, not afraid of anything. He always encouraged him to climb places, to jump from places, etc. He provoked him, and Johnny was fragile, and scared, but he wanted his dad's love so much that he did what was asked of him. I can still see shaking little skinny legs shivering on that ledge. He turned back and said *Look, Dad, I'm doing it*, with a happy grin, but I could see the terror in his eyes. Then he slipped and fell. He didn't die on the spot, and he kept whispering *I did it, Dad, I did it!* I shouted and punched Mike in the hospital. I was more focused on hating him than on my little boy. Hugging that lifeless body for hours at the hospital broke me. I threw Mike out, and I just wanna live my whole life here, mourning for my little perfect boy. That's why I came to this place, so Angela can help me. "
Tara hugged her, unsure how to console her. Unsure also how Angela could help Maggie with her grief. Maggie howled, "Oh, why couldn't I protect him? I could have stopped all that." "It's not your fault," Tara says.

When she got to her room, she saw a tiny bird perched on her desk. She had left her window open. As she closed the door, the bird flew away. She wrote some more half-heartedly, she couldn't fully focus.

Later that evening, Brian approached Tara at the dinner table, and he apologised for behaving a bit strangely. "I want to explain it to you: you look like the spitting image of my wife. She died this year, together with our three children. This is why I was looking at you weirdly, I apologise. She was from Boston, had Irish roots, and red locks like yours."
"That's ok, no harm done! It was just confusing for me," she said awkwardly. "It's a terrible thing to happen to you, I'm really sorry. How are you enjoying the retreat?" she asks, trying to change the subject.
"Well," Brian said, "I can't enjoy anything anymore without them with me, that's why I came here, hoping I can reset and heal as much as possible. What about you? What are you here to heal from?"
"Oh, I came here to write a book," said Tara.
"A book?" He asked, surprised. "Well, whatever works for you," he shrugged. "We all grieve in different ways."
"Oh, I'm not grieving," she said. "I'm quite content with my life. I just want to write my book."
He frowned and stared deep into her eyes.

"Good for you!" he said, sending a shiver of something down her spine.

She sat on the bench under the old oak tree to meditate, counting the acorns fallen on the ground.

~ Day 3 ~

At the retreat, there was no contact with the outside world. Tara found it as tough as she had predicted. But at least some of the people were happy to talk to her, to share their stories. They were probably all writing their life stories, unlike her, who had no real life stories. Nothing interesting had ever happened to her. Except for in her imagination.

Something niggled at her, though. She went to find Angela. She told her some strange coincidences were happening. She had a nightmare and then when she heard Maggie's story, it was very similar to her nightmare. Angela advised her to join her afternoon session that day, as it looked like she should look inside of her, to understand where these thoughts were coming from. Tara wanted to join the session, but as she walked into the room, everyone seemed so sad. She left to get water and didn't return. Instead, she went to her room and started to write. A crow watched her intently from the tree in front of her open window, punctuating the silence with the odd "Craaaw!". She read her story and saw she had written a sad, tragic ending to the love story. She read it again. This wasn't the story she meant to tell, was it? She held Backspace until it was gone, but somehow the heaviness remained in her heart.

The crow cawed again, loudly. She looked up at it. The sound lingered in the still air.

She had asked for her dinner to be brought into her room; she didn't want to stop her writing flow. She now wrote a proper, happy ending. She closed the laptop, sighing contentedly. She noticed her bedside clock had stopped again. Annoyed, she threw it inside the drawer. No point keeping that loser of a clock!

She texted Luke, all was well at home. He had sent a photo of them at the playground. She scanned it thoroughly, looking for dangers or signs things were wrong. It looked like they were doing fine without her, in spite of all the fears that were filling her head before leaving.

Angela brought her a cup of tea. She went to bed early, feeling accomplished. She had made great progress on her stories collection, she thought smiling as she fell asleep, looking at the two cats perched on the outside of her bedroom windowsill.

~ *Day 4* ~

She's pricing some new baby clothes that just came in. She's working at the desk aby the till. She looks up and sees Louise playing with two teddies on the windowsill, outside in the rare sun. She is talking to them cheerfully, brushing her red curls away from her eyes. Her little girl is like a ray of sunshine, always smiling, even when sick. She is the kindest little soul, a proper little mother to her dolls and teddies. Tara's heart swells with pride. She loves it when Louise visits her at the shop, in between preschool and the childminder's. Luke is collecting her in an hour. Tara goes to make a cup of coffee. The shop is quiet, it is lunchtime, and no one will come in now. She heads out back to make her coffee. She hears a huge crashing noise. She runs out and…can't see as her heart stops. A huge truck just crashed into the shop through the window, smashing the wall and the window, and pushing stands towards the till. Her breath stops when she sees Louise's teddy under the truck's wheel, then she sees her girl lying down in a pool of blood. People start coming in, the driver jumps out and calls an ambulance, but he is slurring his words. He was drunk and fell asleep at the

wheel.
Her girl is lifeless, a dribble of blood coming from her temple and another one from the side of her mouth. Her hand is still on her favourite teddy, which is now filling with blood. Tara just shrieks. And shrieks. And shrieks.

Her shrieks woke her up. This nightmare is new, she thinks. The start is familiar, Louise coming to the shop and playing outside. But the accident has never happened; it only happened in her mind for a few seconds as she was looking at her daughter one day.

Tara splashes her face with cold water and goes into the kitchen for a cup of tea. A person she hasn't seen before is there, sitting with a book. "Hi," Tara says, "you're up early." It was 5 a.m.

"Hi, I'm Lotte, I'm from Amsterdam and I've just arrived last night."
"I'm Tara, and I've been here for 3 days. I'm writing a book. Are you here for writing, or for the yoga and meditation workshops?"

"I'm here for the group meditation and healing sessions. I doubt they'll help me. I know I am well beyond help, but my husband made me come here. He thinks I need help, other than the therapy we've both been doing. What about you?"

"I'm here to just write. I will do some yoga sessions, but I don't need the healing or meditation stuff. I've nothing to heal from." She looks out the window and sees an owl just sitting on the back of one of the resort goats. She wants to take a photo, but once she gets her phone up, the owl has disappeared.

"Oh, I have plenty to heal from. Plenty to heal from! Something terrible has happened to our family. Our little girl died in a freak accident last year. She was four and playing just outside our house, in our driveway. We live in a quiet estate in Manchester. Lots of kids running outside on the green, people mowing their lawn, etc. It was a sunny day. I was cleaning the living room windows, so I had them wide open, and I was chatting to Lucy while she was playing with her little ponies in a tub of water with bubbles. She was splashing towards me, giggling. It happened in a split second. I heard a car braking, and then Lucy was thrown up into the air and landed on her back, bumping her head on the cement. She was dead on the spot, the car was doing ninety km an hour. The driver is now in jail as he was drunk, but my baby won't be coming back. I feel so much guilt that I can't go forward. I wanted to kill myself so many times, I just want to go join her. My husband is desperate, he is good but doesn't know how to help me, he thinks this might. One month here in nice weather, organic food, people with similar stories….But I know it won't. I just wanna be with Lucy."

Tara didn't know what to tell Lotte, didn't know how to comfort her. But she felt that story was hers. How could that be? She felt a tightness in her chest when Lotte was talking. She recognised something. She wasn't sure what.

She went to Angela and told her, "I don't know why, but I feel every other writer has had something terrible happen in their lives."
Angela said, "Everyone has a story, in their head or real life. Just listen carefully, you might notice something. Here, there's some calming tea for your evening." She handed her a steaming mug, which smelled of flowers and honey. "It might help with the nightmares," said Angela.
Something in Angela's smile felt like a test.

~ Day 5 ~

She woke up from another nightmare, this one a random one. A guy in a dark tracksuit was chasing her in some woods. She jumped over tree stumps and kept on running. He didn't catch her.

When she woke up, she forgot the dream, but she felt she had dreamt of something important; she tried to remember and shake the strange feeling. Her heart only remembered the fear. She started to relax and write her stories. Another productive day, stopped only by her dipping into the pool at 5 p.m. when the weather wasn't so hot. Maggie was there under a sun umbrella, but she ignored Tara. Tara understood, after all, the woman was grieving. As a mom, it's the worst thing that could happen to you: your kids being gone forever. She is, however, puzzled by the brush-off. It was as if, as soon as Maggie shared her story, she didn't want to talk to Tara anymore. A crow drops a stick in her lap as she was lying by the pool. It startles her, as she was daydreaming.

~ Day 6 ~

She joined a small group for a trip to the village market as it was Saturday. She stayed in the village to walk around a bit. The retreat driver said he'd pick her up again at 8 p.m. She ran into Brian, they had some wine together at the cafe, and she had a sense of déjà vu. The sun was low, the air calm and quiet. Brian was fun, but a bit intense. He just watched her with an unwavering stare, as if he were waiting for something.

"You write love stories with happy endings, right?" he asked, swirling his glass. "I wonder if you still will… after this place."

She goes, "What do you mean?"

He smiled, "Nothing" and looked mysteriously in the distance.

But she couldn't shake the feeling she wasn't writing her stories anymore, that she actually was in one.

~ Day 7~

"He can't breathe," Tara says, agitated, on the phone to her husband. "Come home!" Luke is working in the nearest town, half an hour away from their village in the west of Ireland. Within 25 minutes, he rushes through the door. Eric is pale, a bit damp, his chest rising and falling painfully with a loud wheeze. He is coughing and gasping for air. He is quite limp.
"We need to take him to the hospital," Tara says. They drive, breaking all speed restrictions, and they run through the A&E doors, Luke carrying Eric in his arms. "He's four, he can't breathe," he shouts. They take them straight in, and within minutes, Eric has an oxygen mask, an oxygen monitor, a tube for antibiotics, and they give him steroids. He looks better within minutes, and he

even tries to speak now. They look each other in the eyes with hope. Suddenly, a panicked nurse calls for a doctor. His oxygen levels are dropping, and his blood pressure is falling. Something happened, and they are unsure what. Machines start beeping, doctors push the trolley out of the room, and push the parents aside. Tara has a feeling like a knife inside her heart; she somehow knows she won't see Eric alive again. Suddenly, it all turns black around her.

She woke up in a cold sweat. Oh, it was just a nightmare. She knew Eric was safe at home with Luke.

Later that day, Betty, another retreat guest, shares how her son Rocco died. Betty is from Spain. Her son had asthma. She had asked her husband to refill the prescription, and he stayed out drinking instead. That night, Rocco had a massive attack. She rushed to the hospital, but Rocco died in her arms just as they were getting there. The doctors tried to resuscitate, but he was gone. Betty could never forgive her husband for staying out drinking, or herself for not calling an ambulance. Or if she drove faster… or if they lived closer to the hospital…or…"These regrets are killing me," Betty says.

Tara thought about how it could easily have been her; she thought back to the night Eric was rushed to the hospital. How powerless she felt, how guilty also; she should have taken him to the GP way before he got that bad. *Something was happening here*, she thought. *It felt their stories were her stories. Were they even there? Was the retreat all in her head? What do YOU think?* she asked the owl perched on the roof of the shed. The owl blinked, unbothered.

As she entered her room, she kept feeling that unease. *Was she dreaming their pain, or were they dreaming of hers? Were they here... or was she imagining them?*
She pressed her face against the window. It felt solid and cold. That was real. Wasn't it?

~ Day 8 ~

She went for a long walk in the forest on the ground to clear her mind and advance her book's plot. She found some acorns. She had always liked acorns. As a child, she kept bringing them home, driving her mom mad when she found them in the washing machine. She heard something crack behind her. It was dusk, so it was hard to see, as the trees were covered in shadows. She saw a dark shadow quickly hide behind a tree. She started walking again, thinking whether she should turn back. But no,

Luke always told her if you project fear, it would get worse, so she bravely kept on her track. She heard a noise again. She turned her head and saw a man in a tracksuit running towards her. OMG it was just like in her dream. She started running. Her mind was racing….She stumbled on a root and fell, pain bursting through her ankle. Brian just appeared, lifting her, holding her in his arms for a bit too long. She pushed against him. He hugged her again, his eyes swimming in tears. She felt sorry for him and let him hug her. His lips felt wrong, but also…familiar somehow. Why? How? Oh, he didn't shave in a day or two; his stubble felt just like Luke's. His cologne, too, and the whole feel of him. *This was strange,* she thought. *What the fuck am I doing?* She pushed him strongly.

"I'm sorry," said Brian, "you remind me of my wife."

"Yeah, yeah, you said," she interrupted curtly. She was limping. He heldher by the arm to help. "I don't need your help," she snapped crossly, but in the end, she needed it. They hobbled back to the building together and parted without a word. Angela minded her, put ice on her ankle, and gave her some painkillers and a liquorice-tasting tea from her herbal collection.

I wonder if these teas are what made me have all those dreams, she thought before collapsing into the darkness.

~ Day 9 ~

She avoided everyone, locked in her room like a fortress. She spoke to the crow that appeared sometimes. Now even her phone's time misbehaved. She texted Luke at midnight thinking it was only 9 p.m. She felt embarrassed about letting Brian kiss her. Why were all these people at her writing retreat? They never spoke about their books. They stared at her a lot. They sometimes repeated sentences. She felt sorry for them.

She meditated for hours to stop the shadows, the bad thoughts. It didn't work. She started writing but again all her words were twisted on the screen, they were dark! These were not her words! Has she lost her positive thoughts?

Angela visited her to check on her ankle. Tara was just staring at the wall, not speaking at all, frowning.
Angela said in a low voice, "Tara, you must understand what is happening here."
Tara started "I…I think my nightmares aren't just in my head. I think what I imagined turned real. Somewhere"
Angela said, "Your mind is very powerful. Those stories that you created during some scary

events with your family caused a ripple in other timelines. This retreat exists in between all the timelines, and people from everywhere come here to heal, or to try to stop their nightmares."
Tara widened her eyes. "Are you saying that... those stories of the other guests' kids….I caused that?"
"Their losses are tied to the shadows you created in your mind back then". "How can I stop this? Every time I do something with the kids, I can't stop thinking of the dangers!"
"You have to control your mind. If you let fear consume you, you will tear up more timelines."
"I haven't had those nightmares for years, why now?" Tara asked.
"Because you are at the intersection of all timelines."
"But I can't fix it, I can't go back and not be afraid."
"Yes, but you can stop this from now on. Feed the hope and not the fear!" Angela said.

~ Day 10 ~

Tara felt sick all day, she stayed in bed thinking of all her fears. It really couldn't be that her fears created bad things for all these nice people. She couldn't accept this. She vomited all day, she had a migraine. Light hurt, Even her thoughts hurt.

Angela texted her. She didn't reply. She didn't want her to call over.

The crow was quiet for once, only staring at her through the window all day, but not one sound!

~ Day 11 ~

As this was her last day, Tara went to say goodbye to the others. Everyone told her she could stay with them longer, even forever. "No, I love you all, but this place...I don't belong here," she said. "I don't belong here with you." But she hugged them each close and told them she was sorry. They looked confused, as if they didn't know the whole story.

Brian visited her in her room, hugged her, and begged her to stay with him. "Remember Lake Garda?" he said, "remember how happy you were filming us taking turns driving the speedboat?" Glimpses of her and Louise lying down at the end of the boat on the comfy decking, with their matching anklets, giggling in the sun.
"No, that wasn't me, that was your wife, and your kids!"

Brian looked even more like Luke today, in his

dark blue t-shirt and skinny beige chinos, just like the outfit she got for his birthday. His muscles were even more defined than Luke's. *How had she never noticed how alike they were?*

For a second, she felt tempted to stay longer. But no, she had to go home to her kids. She missed them so much. They were so young, they needed her!

She had to live. She had to stop feeding the shadows.

She got home the next morning, and there was nobody there. She went to the bedroom and collapsed into the bed.
A noise woke her up. She could hear her kids fighting in the room next to hers. Tears sprung to her eyes, she'd never felt so happy hearing them fight. *Oh, what a weird dream that was*, she thought. *It's probably 'cause I wanted to go to that writing retreat, but Luke couldn't handle the kids all alone for that long*, she thought, looking at the brochure of a retreat on her nightstand. It said: *A Writer's Retreat in the French Countryside*. The cover had a photo of a slim woman with high hair, smiling, holding a cup of tea. *Eh, maybe some day*, she thought.

She got out of bed and put on her robe. As she passed the window, the image of the retreat flickered beyond it. She didn't see it.

She rushed to the other room and inhaled the sweet smell of her kids. She hugged them so tight that they squealed and struggled out of her embrace. She felt something in her pocket, and she pulled out a bunch of acorns.
She froze….whatever that place was…maybe it wasn't a dream.

PINK-GLAZED CAKES

The woman comes out of her garden.
"What a lovely child," she says, stroking the golden curls of my son Mason. She's friendly, with her big smile. She's about seventy, dressed in a long pastel floral dress, with a straw hat and red gardener's gloves on.
"Do you live around here?" she smiles at me.
"Yes, on Maple Road," I say.
"What's this guy's name?" she asks.
"Mason."

"Wait a minute," she says, running inside her house. She appears a few seconds later.
"Can I give him a cake?" she asks, holding a plate of cakes.
He smiles on…why is he so happy? He was crying just a minute ago. He seems to like her. He takes the pink-glazed cake from her and eats it. I eat one too. It tastes of summer and roses.
"We have to go," I say. "Does this alley take us to the roundabout?"
"Yes, it is a shortcut through the estate," she says, smiling.

I turned the corner in the alley she had shown me.
I suddenly feel dizzy, would it be the cake? I groggily wonder while I fall to the ground.
I wake up, and I am still in the alley.
No buggy, no Mason.

I ran to the house the woman came out of. I start pounding on the door with both fists.
The woman opens the door. She is wearing the same long floral dress and some white sandals.
"Where's my baby? What did you put in the cake?" I scream.
"What baby?" she asks. "Who are you? What do you want?" she looks confused.
"You gave us cakes," I say. "Don't you remember my Mason? A few minutes ago. You stroked his hair," I say feverishly, my voice pitchy.

She eyes me carefully from head to toe, then says in a gentle voice, "I just got home from town now, see? I was putting my shopping away," she says, pointing to the kitchen counter behind her where a lot of food items were piled high.
"I have never seen you before," she says.
Am I going crazy? Why is she saying she never met me?. The room spins around me.

"Do you want to call someone?" She asks me in a nice, cool voice and hands me her phone. "Sit down here, you look a bit pale," she says, showing

me the armchair in the hallway. "I'll get you a glass of water".
I call my husband.

"Come into the kitchen to wait for him," she says. She makes me a cup of tea and brings a small plate with 2 cakes, pink-glazed cakes. "I just bought these today," she says, "I love them."
My eyes grow wider. It's the cakes! What is happening? My heart pounds.

"You'll be ok," my husband says, rushing in and hugging me. "Thanks for taking care of her," he whispers to the woman.
"What? She put something in our cakes and took Mason and hid him. How can you thank her?" I become more and more agitated. "See, the pink cakes on the plate, it's those!" I scream. "Where is he? What did you do to my boy???" I take her by the shoulders and shake her. My husband gently guides me towards the door.
"You are just confused, honey, you will be ok. You know shouldn't leave the house alone!" he says in a soothing voice.

We walk to the car.

He drives on. He drives to a cemetery. A small black cross. " Mason", it says "30th June 2010 – 28th June 2012."

I remember the date in the paper this morning: 13th July 2013.

CHERUB CURLS

I'm alone. I've been sleeping on the sofa for a week, an ache in my soul.

An empty pill box. I fall into darkness.

A hot tear burns down my cheek. Something stirs next to me. I jerk awake. It's freezing, and I see my wispy breath. A little chubby hand, cherub curls. A small voice, "Momma, I'll come back to you!"

I breathe in his musty toddler smell; it fills my soul, and the ache is gone.

I force myself to the sink, past an angel frame, and puke...puke... puke.

I ring my husband. I breathe another day.

Note to the Reader

Thank you for taking the time to read my stories.

Printed in Dunstable, United Kingdom